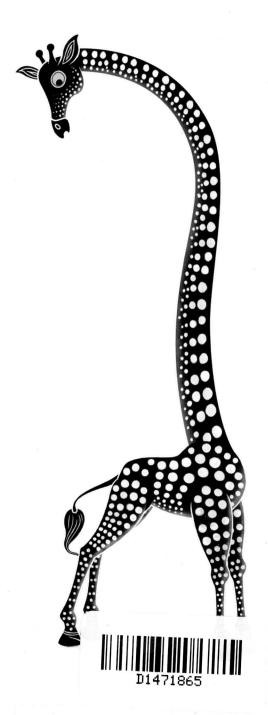

Note to parents and carers

Read it yourself is a series of modern stories, favourite characters and traditional tales written in a simple way for children who are learning to read. The books can be read independently or as part of a guided reading session.

Each book is carefully structured to include many high-frequency words vital for first reading. The sentences on each page are supported closely by pictures to help with understanding, and to offer lively details to talk about.

The books are graded into four levels that progressivel introduce wider vocabulary and longer stories as a reader's ability and confidence grows.

Ideas for use

- Begin by looking through the book and talking about the pictures. Has your child heard this story before?

- Help your child with any words he does not know, either by helping him to sound them out or supplying them yourself.

- Developing readers can be concentrating so hard on the words that they sometimes don't fully grasp the meaning of what they're reading. Answering the puzzle questions on pages 30 and 31 will help with understanding.

For more information and advice on Read it yourself and book banding, visit **www.ladybird.com/readityourself**

Book
Band
5

Level 1 is ideal for children who have received some initial reading instruction. Each story is told very simply, using a small number of frequently repeated words.

Special features:

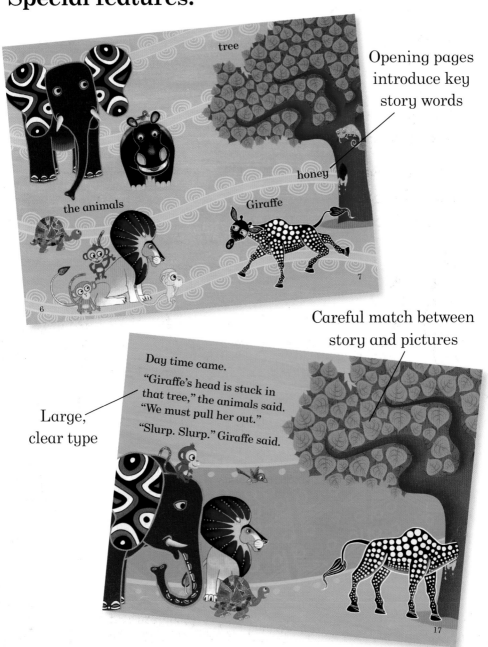

tree

Opening pages introduce key story words

honey

the animals

Giraffe

7

6

Careful match between story and pictures

Day time came.
"Giraffe's head is stuck in that tree," the animals said.
"We must pull her out."
"Slurp. Slurp." Giraffe said.

Large, clear type

17

Tinga Tinga Tales is inspired by
traditional animal stories from Africa
and the Tingatinga artwork of Tanzania

Educational Consultant: Geraldine Taylor
Book Banding Consultant: Kate Ruttle

Created by Claudia Lloyd
Text adapted by Jillian Powell
Illustrations from the TV animation produced
by Tiger Aspect Productions Limited and
Homeboyz Entertainment Kenya
Artwork supplied by Noah Mukono

A catalogue record for this book is available from the British Library

Published by Ladybird Books Ltd
80 Strand, London, WC2R 0RL
A Penguin Company

001

This edition MMXIII

ISBN: 978-0-72327-329-5

Printed in China

Why Giraffe Has a Long Neck

Based on a script by
Edward Gakuya
and Claudia Lloyd

the animals

tree

honey

Giraffe

7

There was a time when Giraffe did not have a long neck or long legs.

There was also a time when Giraffe had an upset tummy.

9

"Honey will help your upset tummy!" the animals said.

There was some honey in the tree. So Giraffe popped her head in the tree.

"Slurp! I love honey!" Giraffe said.

Then Giraffe said,
"I will pull my head
out of the tree now.
Oh help! I am stuck!"

"I can't get my head out,"
Giraffe said. "I am stuck!"

Night time came.

"Slurp. I love honey,"
Giraffe said.

Day time came.

"Giraffe's head is stuck in that tree," the animals said. "We must pull her out."

"Slurp. Slurp." Giraffe said.

So the animals
pulled Giraffe's legs.

"You must not get
upset. We will get
your head out,"
the animals said.

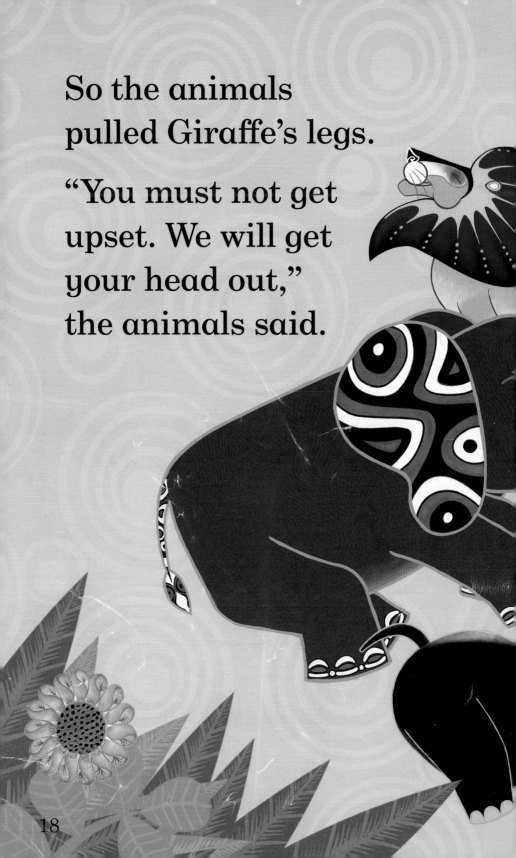

19

A long time went by.

"Now we will also
pull the tree!"
the animals said.

So all the animals
pulled and pulled...

Then the animals said,
"Oh no! Look how long
Giraffe's neck has got!"

More days and nights went by. The tree got taller and taller.

"Look how long Giraffe's neck has got now!" said the animals.

"Giraffe, we can't pull your head now. YOU must pull it," the animals said. "Pull!" Giraffe's head popped out.

"I did it! I am out of the tree!" said Giraffe.

And that is why
Giraffe has a long neck!

How much do you remember about Tinga Tinga Tales: Why Giraffe Has a Long Neck? Answer these questions and find out!

- **What food does Giraffe slurp?**

- **Where is Giraffe's head stuck?**

- **Which animals help get Giraffe out of the tree?**

Look at the pictures from the story and say the order they should go in.

A

B

C

D

Read it yourself with Ladybird

Tick the books you've read!

For children who are ready to take their first steps in reading.

Level 1

 The Enormous Turnip ☐

 Fairy Friends ☐

 Goldilocks and the Three Bears ☐

 Little Red Hen ☐

 The Magic Porridge Pot ☐

 Little Creatures ☐

 Recycling Fun! ☐

 The Princess and the Pea ☐

 Cinderella ☐

 Rex the Big Dinosaur ☐

 The Tale of Peter Rabbit ☐

 The Three Billy Goats Gruff ☐

 Why Giraffe has a Long Neck ☐

 Topsy and Tim Go to the Zoo ☐

 The Ugly Duckling ☐

 The Emperor's New Clothes ☐

For beginner readers who can read short, simple sentences with help.

Level 2

 Beauty and the Beast ☐

 Chicken Licken ☐

 Little Red Riding Hood ☐

 Nature Trail ☐

 Sports Day ☐

 Pirate School ☐

 Rumpelstiltskin ☐

 Sleeping Beauty ☐

 The Gingerbread Man ☐

 ☐

 Sly Fox and Red Hen ☐

 The Tale of Jemima Puddle-Duck ☐

 The Three Little Pigs ☐

 Why Lion Roarrrs! ☐

 Topsy and Tim The Big Race ☐

 Town Mouse and Country Mouse ☐

 Dom's Dragon ☐

 Available on the App Store

The Read it yourself with Ladybird app is now available for iPad, iPhone and iPod touch